Oliver Cat
on Planet B

CHRISTINE KETTNER

DUTTON CHILDREN'S BOOKS

NEW YORK

To my son, Alexander, my one and only

CIP Data is available.

Published in the United States 2003 by Dutton Children's Books,
a division of Penguin Putnam Books for Young Readers
345 Hudson Street, New York, New York 10014
www.penguinputnam.com
Printed in Hong Kong / China   First Edition
ISBN 0-525-47094-8
1 3 5 7 9 10 8 6 4 2

Contents

Oliver Cat Plays a Game

Oliver Cat wanted to play.

Jane Rabbit wanted to play.

"Let's play together,"

they both said.

Oliver Cat said,

"I want to play hopscotch!"

Jane Rabbit said,

"I don't want to play hopscotch.

I want to play cards."

Oliver Cat said,

"I don't want to play cards.

I want to play tic-tac-toe."

Jane Rabbit said,

"I don't want to play tic-tac-toe.

I want to play checkers."

Oliver Cat said,

"I don't want to play checkers.

I want to play marbles."

Jane Rabbit said,

"I don't want to play marbles.

I want to jump rope."

Oliver Cat said,

"I don't want to jump rope.

I want to fly a kite."

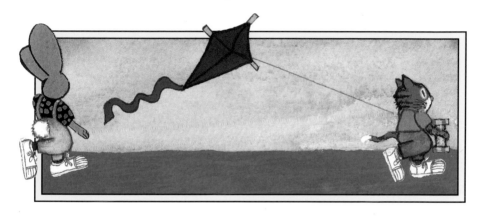

Jane Rabbit said,

"I don't want to fly a kite.

I want to play hide-and-seek."

"Suppertime!"

their mothers called.

Oliver Cat went home.

Jane Rabbit went home.

"Bye," they both said.

"We'll play a new game tomorrow."

Oliver Cat Loses a Button

Oliver Cat lost a button

on his shirt.

He was late for school.

He went next door

to his friend Charles Crocodile.

"Mr. Crocodile," asked Oliver Cat,

"do you have a button for my shirt?"

"No," said Charles Crocodile.

"But I can give you this old radio.

Ask Brenda Mouse next door."

"Ms. Mouse," asked Oliver Cat,

"do you have a button for my shirt?"

"No," answered Brenda Mouse.

"But I can give you this eggbeater.

Ask Paul Puffin next door."

"Mr. Puffin," asked Oliver Cat,

"do you have a button for my shirt?"

"No," answered Paul Puffin.

"But I can give you this old bicycle.

Ask Rosie Rabbit next door."

"Mrs. Rabbit," asked Oliver Cat,

"do you have a button for my shirt?"

"No," answered Rosie Rabbit.

"But I can give you this old fan.

Ask Helen Hedgehog next door."

"Ms. Hedgehog," asked Oliver Cat,

"do you have a button for my shirt?"

"No," answered Helen Hedgehog.

"But I can give you this broken-down

TV set."

Oliver Cat

did not think

this was the way to get his button.

He took

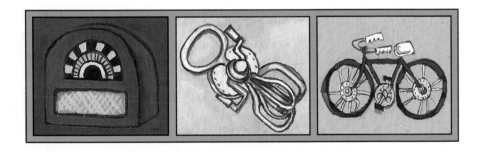

the radio, the eggbeater, the bicycle,

the fan, the TV set, and some other old junk.

He built a spaceship.

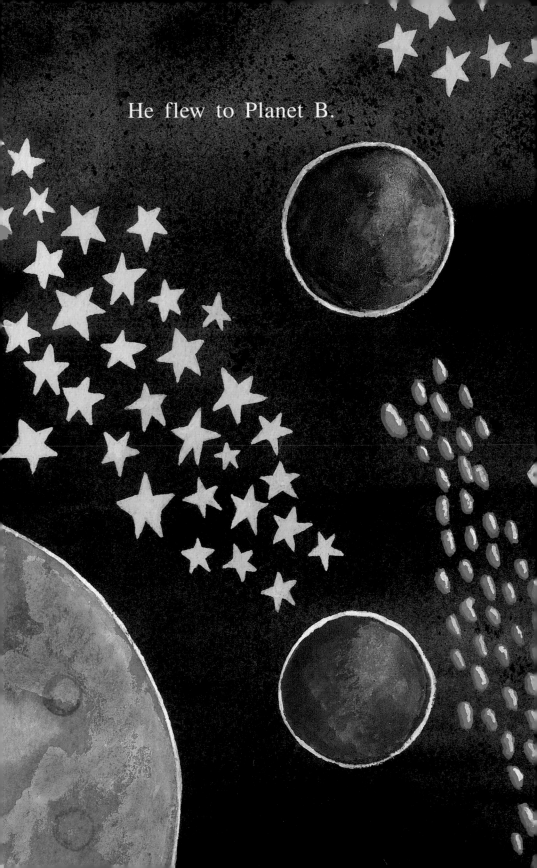

He flew to Planet B.

"Greetings,"

said a space creature.

"Mr. Space Creature," asked Oliver Cat,

"do you have a button for my shirt?"

"Yes," said the space creature.

"You have come to Planet B.

It is the Planet of Buttons.

Help yourself."

Oliver Cat found

just the right button.

"Thank you," he said.

"And good-bye."

Oliver Cat

flew home.

"Did you find a button for your shirt?"

asked Charles Crocodile.

"Yes, I did.

But I'm really late now,"

said Oliver Cat.

He ran off to school.

"Oliver Cat,

why are you late this time?"

asked his teacher.

"I lost a button on my shirt,"

said Oliver Cat.

Oliver Cat Goes Fishing

Oliver Cat stood on the dock.

He was fishing.

The sun was hot.

The sky was blue.

So was the ocean.

He thought about what

he would catch and cook.

He was hungry.

Oliver Cat sat still.

His fishing line was quiet.

Then he felt a tug.

The fishing line went tug-tug again.

Oliver Cat pulled and pulled.

A pink spotted fish came out of the

blue ocean.

She was a ballet-dancing fish.

She held out her fins and danced

on tippy-tail.

Oliver Cat could not

eat a fish like this.

He threw the pink spotted fish

back into the blue ocean.

Oliver Cat sat still.

His fishing line was quiet.

Then he felt a tug.

The fishing line went tug-tug again.

Oliver Cat pulled and pulled.

An orange lobster came out

of the blue ocean.

He was a tap-dancing lobster.

He went tap-de-tap with his claws.

Oliver Cat could not eat

a lobster like this.

He threw the orange lobster

back into the blue ocean.

Oliver Cat sat still.

His fishing line was quiet.

Then he felt a tug.

The fishing line went tug-tug again.

Oliver Cat pulled and pulled.

A silver mermaid cat came out

of the blue ocean.

This mermaid cat

played the cello.

She went r-r-r-r-r-r-r-r-r

on the strings of her cello.

Oliver Cat could not eat

a mermaid cat like this.

He threw the mermaid cat

and her cello

back into the blue ocean.

The sun was setting.

The sky was changing.

The ocean was getting darker.

Oliver Cat's fishing basket

was empty.

He was hungry.

Oliver Cat thought that

a cheese sandwich on brown bread

would be a very good supper.